Emmy
the Exaggerating
Elephant

Fenton
the Fearful Frog

Gertie
the Grungy Goat

the Happy
Hamster

the Impatient
Iguana

Ollie
the Obedient
Ostrich

Perry
the Polite
Porcupine

Queenie
the Quiet Quail

Rupert
the Resourceful
Rhinoceros

Wendy
the Wise
Woodchuck

Xavier
the X-ploring
Xenops

Yori
the Yucky Yak

Ziggy
the Zippy Zebra

NOTE TO PARENTS

<u>Tina Tells the Truth</u>
A story about tactfulness

In this story, Tina the Truthful Tiger tells the truth in a way that hurts her friends' feelings. With the help of the AlphaPets, Tina finds out how to tell the truth in a friendly and thoughtful way.

In addition to enjoying this story with your child, you can use it to teach a gentle lesson about being sensitive of others' feelings—being *tactful.* Help your child understand that the truth is important, but how you tell the truth is important, too.

You can also use this story to introduce the letter **T**. As you read about Tina the Truthful Tiger, ask your child to listen for all the words that start with **T** and point to the objects that begin with **T**. When you've finished reading the story, your child will enjoy doing the activity at the end of the book.

The AlphaPets™ characters were conceived and created by Ruth Lerner Perle.
Characters interpreted and designed by Deborah Colvin Borgo.
Cover/book design and production by Norton & Company.
Logo design by Deborah Colvin Borgo and Nancy S. Norton.

Printed and Manufactured in the United States of America

Tina
Tells the Truth

RUTH LERNER PERLE

Illustrated by Judy Blankenship

Grolier Enterprises Inc.,   Danbury, Connecticut

One Tuesday morning, Tina the Truthful Tiger met Katy the Kind Koala riding on the bus.

"Good morning, Tina!" Katy said. "Where are you going today?"

"I'm going downtown to have my typewriter fixed," Tina said.

"I'm going that way too," Katy said. "I need to buy cookies for our Wednesday get-together at Wendy's house."

When the bus came to their stop, Tina and Katy got off and walked toward Rupert's Rapid Repair Shop.

On the way, they passed the Hats Galore store. Emmy the Exaggerating Elephant was inside trying on a great big feathery hat trimmed with red taffeta tulips, purple ruffles, and green tinsel. Tina and Katy went inside.

"Hello! Hello!" Emmy called to them. "Don't you think this hat looks divine on me?"

Tina looked at Emmy. "Well, the truth is, it looks more like a mistake than a hat," she said. "You look silly."

Emmy's eyes filled with tears.

"Don't cry, Emmy," Katy said. "Tina didn't mean to hurt your feelings. She only meant that she likes plain hats better."

"Well, do *you* think I look good in this hat?" Emmy asked Katy.

Katy pointed to another hat. "How about trying on that pink one? It's not as frilly, and it matches the color of your dress," she suggested.

Emmy tried the pink hat. "You're right, Katy. This hat *does* look better! I'll buy it," Emmy said with a smile. She gave Katy a big hug and thanked her for being so kind and helpful. But Emmy said nothing to Tina.

"What did I do wrong?" Tina wondered. She felt a funny feeling at the bottom of her heart. "I tried to be helpful, too, but Emmy seems upset with me."

When they left the hat store, Katy waved good-bye to
Tina and said, "I hope to see you at Wendy's tomorrow!"

"I'll be there," Tina said, as she ran off to Rupert's
Rapid Repair Shop.

When Tina got to the shop, she looked around at all the broken things—TV sets, telephones, toasters, tennis rackets, tapedecks, and trunks. Everything was topsy-turvy and covered with dust.

Tina handed her typewriter to Rupert the Resourceful Rhinoceros and explained what was wrong with it.

"I'll have this fixed for you in a jiffy," he said. "You can pick it up tomorrow after lunch."

"Maybe you can have this place tidied up by then, too! It's a terrible mess, Rupert, and that's the truth," Tina said.

Tina continued talking about other things, but Rupert wasn't listening. He just stared and didn't say a word.

Finally, Tina said, "What's wrong, Rupert? You don't seem your usual cheery self."

Rupert felt embarrassed, but he was angry, too.

"You know, Tina," he said, "most broken things can be fixed. And some things are easier to fix than others. But the hardest thing to fix is hurt feelings."

Rupert came out from behind the counter. "I have to get to work now," he said. He showed Tina to the door and quickly closed it behind her.

The next afternoon, Tina went to pick up her typewriter. She was hoping Rupert would be in a better mood. Along the way, she passed Lizzy the Lazy Lamb standing near her vegetable garden. Lizzy was looking very upset.

"What's wrong?" Tina asked.

"I forgot to water my garden, and now all my vegetables are wilted. Just look at these turnips and tomatoes!" Lizzy cried.

"Well, the truth is, it's your own fault. You shouldn't be so lazy, Lizzy," said Tina.

"Humm, I guess you're right," Lizzy said, and she turned to go inside her house.

Just then, Perry the Polite Porcupine passed by.

"Good afternoon," he said. "Looks like your garden could use some water, Lizzy. If you'll get your hose, I'll help you try to revive your plants."

Lizzy smiled a big smile. "Oh, Perry! That would be wonderful!" she said. Lizzy took Perry by the hand, and together they went to get the hose.

"What did I do wrong?" Tina wondered. "Now Lizzy is upset with me." Once again Tina felt that funny feeling at the bottom of her heart.

When Tina got to Rupert's shop, she noticed that it was neat and clean.

"Well! Well!" she said. "This place looks terrific now, and that's the truth!"

"I thought about what you said," declared Rupert. "It was true that my shop was a mess. I cleaned it up, and it really does look much better now. I'm glad you told me the truth, Tina, but I still don't like the *way* you told me."

Tina felt confused and unhappy, but she said nothing. "The truth is the truth," she thought to herself as she paid Rupert. "How else can I say it?"

Rupert handed Tina her typewriter and she left.

Carrying her typewriter, Tina walked through the park
and sat down on a bench by the lake. Tears came to her
eyes as she tried to figure out what she was doing
wrong. She had that awful funny feeling at the bottom of
her heart again.

"I'm supposed to tell the truth. Everyone knows that,"
she thought. "But why does it make me feel so bad?"

Just then, Wendy passed by on her way home from the
supermarket. She saw Tina sitting alone and looking sad.

"Tina, what's wrong?" she asked.

"I don't know," Tina said. "It's all very confusing. I know it's right to tell the truth, but when I do, everyone gets upset with me."

Wendy sat down and thought for a while. Then she said, "Telling the truth is very important. But sometimes the truth alone is not enough. It's not only what you say that counts. How you say it counts, too. That's called using *tact*."

"How can I get some tact?" Tina asked.

"Easy! Just tell the truth in a kind way," Wendy explained. "For instance, if someone gives you a present that you don't really want, don't say 'Yuck! This is awful!' or 'I already have one.' Say, 'Thank you very much for your thoughtfulness.' Or if someone is wearing a funny-looking coat, don't point and laugh. Remember, if you have nothing nice to say, it's usually better not to say anything at all."

Wendy picked up her packages. "Now dry your eyes, Tina, and come home with me," she said. "You can help me get everything ready for this afternoon."

Together, the two friends walked to Wendy's house.

Tina helped Wendy lay out a tray of cookies, cinnamon toast, and tea.

Soon Katy and Perry arrived along with Herbie the Happy Hamster, Albert the Absent-minded Alligator, and Ziggy the Zippy Zebra.

Everyone talked and had fun. After a while, Wendy took out her clarinet and played a tune. Katy accompanied her on the piano and Herbie played his tuba.

Herbie followed along as best he could, but his tuba growled and groaned. Tina was tempted to cover her ears, but she didn't. She remembered what Wendy said, and didn't want to hurt Herbie's feelings.

"That must be tact," she said to herself.

While they were playing, Herbie leaned over to Tina and said, "Maybe I shouldn't join in. I know I don't play very well."

Tina thought a minute, then she said, "Don't stop playing, Herbie. You're sure to improve if you just keep on practicing."

Wendy heard what Tina said to Herbie.

"Hooray! You've just passed the tact test!" she whispered in Tina's ear. "Now, Tina, you're not only a truthful tiger, but a tactful tiger, too!"

Everyone clapped for the musicians when they finished playing, but Tina couldn't help thinking that the applause was also for her.

Tina felt wonderful, and now the bottom of her heart felt wonderful, too.

To tell the truth, these are terrific words.

table

teapot

telephone

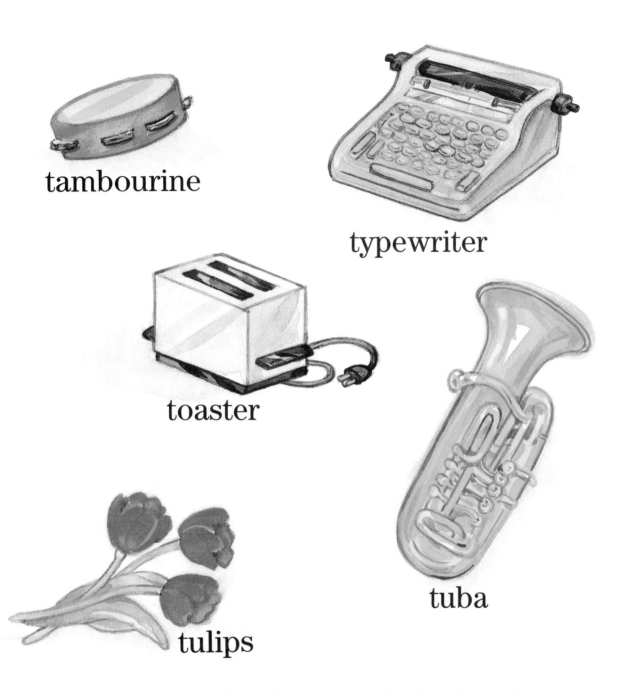

tambourine

typewriter

toaster

tuba

tulips

Look back at the pictures in this book, and find these and other words that begin with T.

Aa Bb

Gg Hh

Mm Nn Oo Pp

Uu Vv Ww